# This book belongs to

# For Deborah and Scarlett

Dorling **DK** Kindersley

LONDON, NEW YORK, SYDNEY, DELHI, PARIS,
MUNICH and JOHANNESBURG

First published in Great Britain in 2000
by Dorling Kindersley Limited,
9 Henrietta Street, London WC2E 8PS

2 4 6 8 10 9 7 5 3 1

Text and illustrations copyright © 2000 Melanie Walsh
The author's and illustrator's moral rights have been asserted.

A CIP catalogue record for this book is available from the British Library.

ISBN 0-7513-7267-6

Colour reproduction by Dot Gradations, UK
Printed in China by South China Press

see our complete
catalogue at
**www.dk.com**

# Ned's Rainbow

## melanie Walsh

A Dorling Kindersley Book

Ned loves rainbows.

He wears a
rainbow
hat. . .

rainbow
pyjamas. . .

and
rainbow
socks.

But Ned has never ever seen
a real rainbow.

Until one rainy day when Ned is playing in the park. All of a sudden the sun starts to shine and a beautiful rainbow appears across the sky.

"**WOW!**" Ned shouts
as he runs towards
the lovely soft colours.

Ned runs up and down

and round and round and round the park,

but he can't catch the rainbow.

He cries all the way home,
all the way through dinner,
and he even refuses to wear
his rainbow pyjamas to bed!

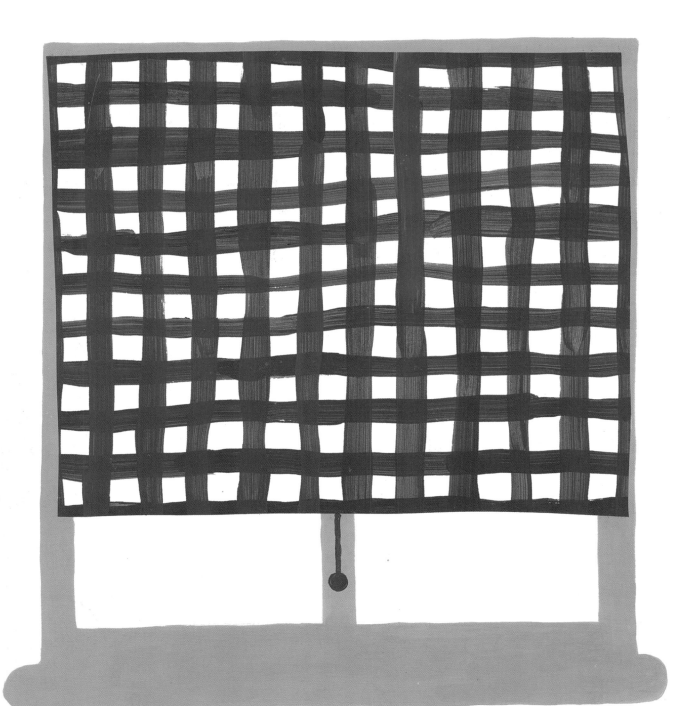

When Ned wakes up the next morning, he doesn't look at the sky. He just goes straight to playgroup with a long, sad face.

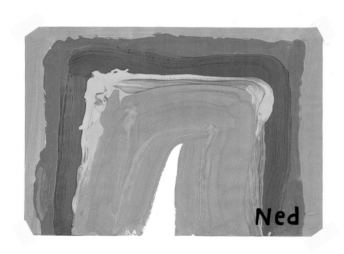

Ned

violet

indigo

Ned is still sad when he comes home. He slowly climbs the stairs to his bedroom and opens the door.

red

yellow

green

blue

orange

"my very own rainbow!" shouts Ned.

So now when Ned wakes
see and touch his

up every morning, he can

very own rainbow.

But he still looks
out of the window
for real ones!

# Other Toddler Books to collect:

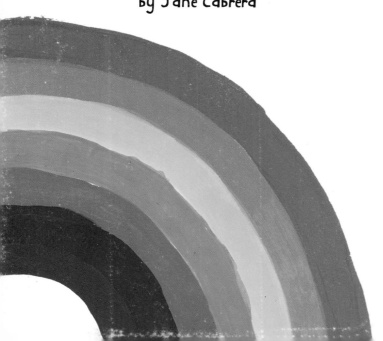